AF582044

Cellgineer:

A Poetic Tale

Leon X

Disclaimer:

This is a work of poetry. It is a story conjured by the imagination and intellect of the author. This is a work of fiction. Names, characters, businesses, places, events and incidents are either the products of the author's imagination or used in a fictitious manner. Any resemblance to actual persons, living or dead, or actual events is purely coincidental.

Author's Note:

I, the author, Leon X, do not promote any of these actions done through this poetic tale, nor promote any other actions expressed through any of my works under Leon X, both in poetics and/or in novels.

Thank you for understanding.

- Leon X

Poetic Tale:

Meet Lio, a cellular engineer, also known as the Cellgineer. Lio, being a master in his scientific craft, has already crafted bones, organs, and even full body suits of skin through his cellular engineering principles and discoveries. Now, he wants to do the real deal.

Lio uses all of his biological and cellular engineering knowledge and expertise and forms a full-fledged adult male. Yet something is of missing and he does not know of what. Lio knows the biological and the cellular placements are correct and active, and his medical devices of the highest order are showing signs of life but something is of missing. Lio expresses himself in word to figure it out.

Yet, the real question is, what if what Lio is really missing for his final work is actually within him?

"Does not all start within the Cell?"

- Leon X

Cellgineer Lio

1

Is it not of Thy!

A'ha!

It hath been done!

2

Am Thy not of the Gods?!
Or are the Gods of Thy?
The cells...

3

Of the mi'nute,
Into tissue,
And into full fledg'd organ,

4

Both of the mi'nute,
And of the mass!
And a'now,

<u>*5*</u>

A full fledge of life,
Yet...
It appeareth not to moveth as of yet,

6

Although breathing,
And of activity of electrical signals of the brain,
As all organs Thy formed through cellular
engineering be of the functioning tu',

7

And of flesh visible to touch within the three,

Yet...

No movement?

8

Strange...

Am Thy not the finest cellular engineer of tis' world?!

Or possibly of tis' galaxy whom is of continuous spin?!

9

Possibly with'in the universe of the physical?
Are not cells of life?
And form'd into tissue?

10

Then into the complexity of living organ?
Or are they only the complexity of a single cell,
And only given full ex'pression at the large scale?

11

As the cell itself knoweth what to doeth,
HA!
The cell's full ex'pression is of the organ,

12

The muscle of red,
The nerve of yellow and of white,
The vessels of blue and of red,

13

And of the layers of skin,
Thy am only to ponder...
And pondering is to giveth answer,

14

As a cell itself is of ex'press'd in either the minute
and of the mass,
It must be,
Yet perhaps...

15

Thy specimen of flesh,
In front of Thy,
And Thy alone...

16

Within Thy lab of secret,
Of tubes,
Glass,

17

And of light,
Such orderly within Thy lab for Thy and Thy alone,
Thy lab of the Highest...

18

Unrivalled by none,
Not even countries...
Hahaha!

<u>19</u>

Cellular division upon dissection tables,
And anatomical wunders both on table and hung and cleanse'd through chemical,
And of yet...

20

There is of something missing...
Cells are of the genius itself,
They knoweth what to do...

21

As Thy am to knoweth what to do with they,
Yet...
They are of Thy,

22

And Thy am of them,
Alas with this type of ponder,
Thy must let it rest,

23

The cells knoweth what to do,
Thy am only to placeth,
Over the frame Thy craft'd,

<u>24</u>

Yet...
Something is of missing,
Be it breath?

25

Life?
Or of Spirit?
Yet...

26

What is it?!
All cells ex'pressed and forme'd,
Ex'pressed...

27

Into marrow,
Bone,
Nerve,

28

Into muscle,
Organ,
Vessel,

29

Into liquidous ex'change,
Into gaseous and physical ex'change,
The ex'panding and of the re'tracting,

30

And of the process of pain and of pleasure,
Faster than the speed of thought,
And of the speed of all physical light as of a'now,

31

And of life...
And only life is of the biological,
The essence of life...

32

Yet be not that of a cell?
Nor of an organ?
Nor of the whole?

33

Perhaps...
Thy re'created all cells,
And divided into the plenty,

34

Cells that contain'th their own code themselves,
Into mass tissue and of living organs,
And place'd within the sculptural frame firmly,

35

Of the adult male,
And of yet...
Thy am of missing...

36

Of something that maketh Thy to wunder within the space of mind...

Could it be that what Thy am of missing is beyond of cells?

And beyond the biology of the physical?

37

Bio-electrical?

As with the tissue of those of the spirit and aspects of the physical mind?

Or am Thy only to knoweth not...

38

Am Thy not of the Gods?!
The cells work'th themselves,
As the lungs are to inhale'th,

39

As the brain is to be of active,
As the heart is to beat in natural rhythm of the safe,
As blood is to process through both the red and of
blue vessels knowingly,

40

Broken down into cells of round themselves as of liquid to nourish,
The organs knoweth themselves as Nature herself,
Yet...

<u>**41**</u>

Strange...
As Thy am to wunder wunce a'more,
Upon tis' phenomena...

42

Cells do not govern the psychological,
Yet receptors there are,
Yet they be of cells themselves,

43

Yet craft no personality without ex'perience,
Nor genetics,
Nor cultures,

44

Nor influence of the society or of peoples around,

Yet...

Is psychology within the cells?

45

Hmph…

Psychology…

Thy am only to get'th off track,

46

Cells?
Cellular engineer…
To craft a liver,

47

Thy can do,
To craft another brain of flesh,
Thy can do,

48

To craft another heart with the specific bioelectrical tissue,
Thy can do,
Yet to maketh Man fully,

49

And of pure functional essence...
Thy am in stuck...
For is it...?

<u>50</u>

Is it so...?
That the Spirit is beyond cells?
Thy am to know'th...

51

A-Ha!

Eureka! So they sayeth,

May the Angels sing'th praises in Thy name!

52

Thy breath,
Into the breath of Thy creation,
And a'now!

53

The cells of flesh ex'pressed in the plethora of forms,
Yet masterly placed,
By the Master Engineer and Sculptor himself,

<u>**54**</u>

Am Thy not only a student?!
Thy creation of cellular multiplication to mass
ex'pression,
IS OF NOW ALIVE!

55

ALIVE!

It breathes and of blinks!

Strange...!

__56__

Thy was only to follow the formulae of cells,
The plethora of cells within the system of Man,
And of the dissection of each under the scope,

57

And the growth of each cell ex'pressed to full
working colored organ,
And live organs functioning together within all,
Through and only through the set of fully ex'pressed
cells of the visible form as of a'now,

58

This cannot be of real!
There is no one to shareth Thy joy...
Yet...

<u>*59*</u>

This must be Thy responsibility,
Cellular division and multiplication into a new
fledged man of living!
Yet...

60

With the vastness of unique cells,
In term of shape,
Placement over each,

61

And complexity of division,
Both of the attack and of the defense...
Thy am only to use'th the blueprints,

62

Given by science,

Yet,

What is it that charges the cells?

<u>63</u>

Breath unto breath?
And a'now,
The specimen is of fully alive,

64

Yet,
The cells are to worketh to keep'th a'live,
Yet...

<u>65</u>

All of tis' is given by the building blocks of science,
And of yet,
Thy feel'th it is not only science a'lone,

<u>66</u>

Perhaps,

By whom?

Could it not be the Creator Himself or of the Devil?

67

Is it to be of said?
That Thy creat'd an image of Thyself into Man,
Through cellular engineering,

68

And through cellular engineering a'lone?

Yet...

Whom was to giveth the blueprint of it all?

69

Science?
Or was it of the Holy God?
Or of the Devil?

<u>70</u>

Or was it truly of Thyself?

End.

About the Author

Leon X is a novelist and poet.

Visit www.leonxtheauthor.com for more information on the author.

Thank you for supporting.

Other Works by Leon X

Poetic Collections & Tales:

Luthier

Kalibal

The Gate

Sacrifice'th

Talisman of Zeus

Escape from the Madhouse

Limbs for Use

Wrath of I'Kan

Unlocking the Below

& More

Novels:

Disbelief

Comp-Passion

Gloom to Bloom

KALI

www.ingramcontent.com/pod-product-compliance
Lightning Source LLC
LaVergne TN
LVHW041130150826
845673LV00007B/2259